# Montgomery's
# TIME ZONE

## C. A. Nobens

Carolrhoda Books, Inc./Minneapolis

*For Tom Montgomery,*
*who's never been on time*
*for anything that I know of.*
*Nevertheless, his value as my old friend*
*keeps right up*
*with the passing of years.*

Copyright © 1990 by C. A. Nobens

Library of Congress Cataloging-in-Publication Data

Nobens, C.A.
Montgomery's time zone / C.A. Nobens
p.   cm.
Summary: Montgomery the duck decides to create his own time zone so he will not have to worry about being on time, but he soon realizes that if everyone keeps his own time it might ruin his birthday.
ISBN 0-87614-398-2 (lib. bdg.)
[1. Ducks—Fiction.  2. Time—Fiction.  3. Birthdays—Fiction.]  I. Title.
PZ7.N664Mo   1990
[E]—dc20                                                          89-17388
CIP
AC

Manufactured in the United States of America
1  2  3  4  5  6  7  8  9  10  00  99  98  97  96  95  94  93  92  91  90

**M**ontgomery knew all about telling time. He knew about big hands and little hands. He knew about digital clocks. He even knew how to dial the right number on the telephone to hear the time.

But there was one thing Montgomery didn't understand— what was all the fuss about being *on* time?

Every morning Montgomery's Mom called out from the foot of the stairs, "Time to get up, Montgomery!"

It never seemed like that time to Montgomery.
To him, it always felt much more like time to go back to sleep.
Finally, though, he always had to get up.
And then he had to hurry like crazy to catch the school bus.
Sometimes he even had to eat his toast on the run.

Montgomery thought many kinds of times were just plain wrong: time for arithmetic at school, time for homework, bath time, time to visit Aunt Betty.

"Why can't *I* decide when it's time to get up, or time to go to school, or anything?" Montgomery grumbled to himself almost every day. "What's the big deal about being on time anyhow?"

**T**hen, on the day before Montgomery's birthday,
there was an envelope in the mailbox addressed to him.
At first glance, Montgomery was thrilled.
"It's a birthday card for me! For me!" he gabbled excitedly.

He tore the envelope open.  Inside was a card that read:

*It's time for your dental checkup.*
*Signed,*
*Dr. Noah Caviti*
Your Dentist

Montgomery was so disappointed that
he threw the card on the ground and stomped all over it.
"I've had it with time-for-this's and time-for-that's!" he squawked.

Montgomery made up his mind.
"As a present for my birthday,"
he promised himself, "I'm going to
start up my own private time zone.
I'll call it **M**ontgomery **S**tandard **T**ime...
**MST** for short. Then I'll be able to do
everything when *I* think it's time—not when
everybody *else* thinks it is!"

**T**hat night, Montgomery's Dad said, "Time for bed, son."

Montgomery trotted off with a smile. He didn't mind because it wasn't really bedtime *(MST)*—it was time to watch the Friday night late movie. And **M**ontgomery **S**tandard **T**ime would go into effect the very next day. That wasn't long to wait!

As he climbed into bed, Montgomery imagined himself watching the Saturday Midnight Monster Movie. He felt very clever.

Snuggling into his pillows, Montgomery thought happily, "Tomorrow is my birthday! I hope it's every bit as wonderful as my last one!"

Last year, Montgomery remembered, his Mom had fixed him his favorite breakfast—blueberry waffles. His Dad had taken him downtown to Al's Sporting Goods Store and let him pick out a new catcher's mitt. Back at home again, he'd found all of his friends waiting to surprise him with a big birthday party.

After *that*, his Grandma and Grandpa had taken him to a movie and bought him popcorn and a giant strawberry pop.

Montgomery wriggled deeper into his comfy quilt, smiling drowsily. Two big yawns later, he closed his eyes. Before he knew it, he was asleep.

$S$uddenly, Montgomery's eyes flew open.
The sun streamed through his windows.
"It's my birthday!" he cried. "I wonder why Mom didn't call me?"
He jumped out of bed and sniffed the air for blueberry waffles.
Not a whiff came to tickle his bill.

Montgomery ran down the stairs.
"Hi, Mom!" he shouted.
"I'm ready for my Happy Birthday Breakfast!"

"Already?" asked his Mom in surprise.
She was reading the newspaper and drinking coffee.

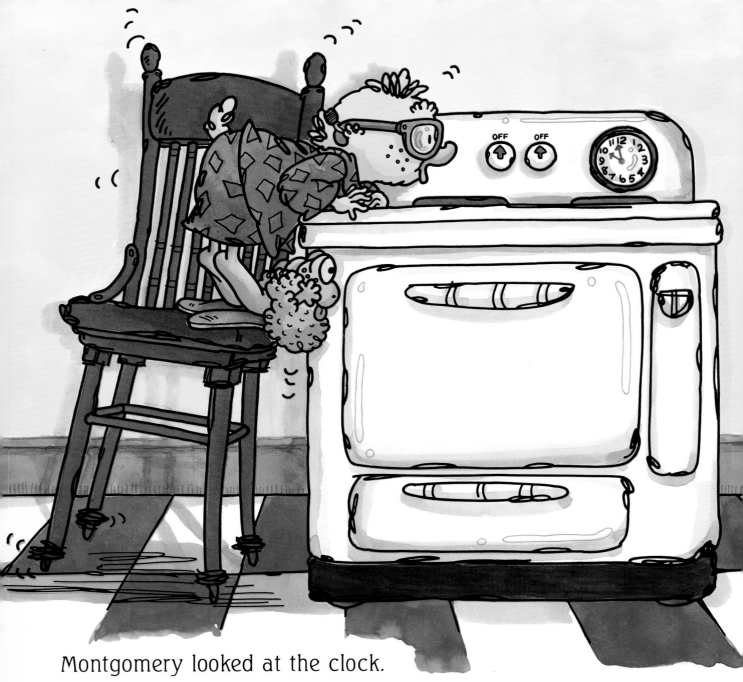

Montgomery looked at the clock.
"Well, yes!  Already!" he sputtered. "It's practically ten o'clock!"

"Not according to *my* time," his Mom said, looking at
her wristwatch. "It's just after 6 a.m. *M*other *P*acific *T*ime."

"But, but..." Montgomery stammered, "it's my birthday
and I'm hungry and I thought you'd make me my blueberry waf—"
Montgomery stopped, startled by thumping footsteps.

Montgomery's Dad barged noisily into the kitchen, wearing his coat and hat. "Ready to go? Good!" he trumpeted. "No time to dawdle!"

"Go?" asked Montgomery.

"Yes, go!" he cried, flinging the door open, "To Al's Sporting Goods Store to pick out your present!"

Montgomery began to whine. "But I haven't had any breakfast! And I have on my pajamas!"

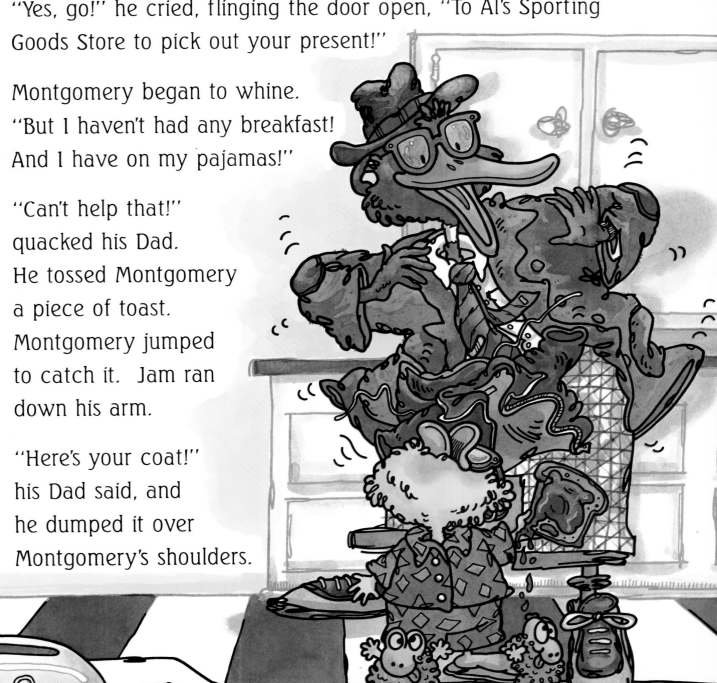

"Can't help that!" quacked his Dad. He tossed Montgomery a piece of toast. Montgomery jumped to catch it. Jam ran down his arm.

"Here's your coat!" his Dad said, and he dumped it over Montgomery's shoulders.

In the car, Montgomery's Dad pointed to the clock on the dashboard. "Look at that!" he crowed with satisfaction. "We're right on time."

"Ten-oh-five?" Montgomery read, baffled.

"Not according to **F**ather **C**entral **T**ime," his Dad said, beaming. "It's a quarter to nine. Just time enough to get to Al's Sporting Goods as it opens for business."

Montgomery gnawed at his cold, runny toast.
He was very disappointed in it, having expected blueberry waffles.
He felt goofy going downtown in his pajamas and slippers too.

His Dad parked the car in front
of Al's Sporting Goods Store.
He plunked money in the meter and waved to Montgomery.
"Come on, son!" he called.
"It's time to pick out your birthday present!"

Montgomery felt a little bit better
at the thought of his present.
He slid out of the car and hurried to the store entrance.

His Dad pulled on the door handle.
But the door was locked.
He looked at his wristwatch.
"Funny!" said Montgomery's Dad.  "It's nine o'clock sharp!"

Montgomery looked at the sign on the door.  It read:

AL'S SPORTING GOODS
HOURS
DAILY: 9 a.m. to 5 p.m.
*Al's* *Mountain* *Time*

"Oh, no!" groaned Montgomery.
"We might as well just go home.
Who *knows* when *Al's* *Mountain* *Time* is."

On the way home, Montgomery tried hard to console himself. He felt very much like crying. No special breakfast! No present from Al's Sporting Goods Store! He sniffled a little. "At least," he told himself bravely, "there will be my birthday party."

**B**ut when Montgomery and his Dad walked into
the kitchen, his Mom was still reading the newspaper.
There was no sign at all of any of his friends, or a cake,
or streamers, or hats and horns. Montgomery went
to the refrigerator and peered unhappily into the freezer.
There wasn't even any ice cream in there.

"Where's my birthday party?"
Montgomery wailed at the top of his lungs.

"Oh, goodness!" his Mom said,
pouring herself another cup of coffee.
"I suppose it's almost time to send out invitations, isn't it?"

Montgomery stared
at his Mom.
Montgomery stared
at his Dad.
Then he ran into the den.
Frantically, he dialed his
grandparent's phone
number.

After two or three rings,
his Grandpa said,
"Hello?"

"Grandpa-Grandpa-this-is-Montgomery," babbled Montgomery, all flustered. "What time are you coming over to take me to my birthday movie?"

"Why, Montgomery, dear," said his Grandpa with a chuckle, "your birthday's not until *next* month. I'm looking at the calendar on my digital watch this very minute."

Montgomery stared at the telephone.
He began to feel quite odd.
A voice from somewhere
very far away seemed
to be saying
"It's time…
It's time…"

All of a sudden,
Montgomery
sat up in bed.

"**I**t's time to get up!" his Mom was calling from downstairs. "It's time for blueberry waffles!"

In a flash, Montgomery jumped out of bed. He sniffed the sweet smell of hot waffles. "Mmmmmmmmm," he grinned.

As he pulled his T-shirt over his head, he muttered, "*M*ontgomery *S*tandard *T*ime…what a stupid idea!"

He buckled up his overalls. "I'm getting dressed, MOM," Montgomery hollered, "I'll be there just as soon as I put on my watch!"

One minute later, *exactly*, he ran down the stairs to start his special day.

(He had a great time.)